Terrible Things Live in the Fear Street Woods.

People have seen all sorts of scary creatures. Ghosts. Ghouls. Even monsters. Every night horrifying howls and moans come from the deep woods just behind Dylan Brown's house.

And Dylan couldn't be happier about it. He's always wanted to see a ghost, and when his father clears out a part of the woods it looks as if he'll get his chance.

He and his brother Steve found an old tree house in the clearing. One that's supposed to be haunted. So the two of them are going to spend the night there.

Dylan is ready to come face to face with a ghost . . .

Are you?

STAY AWAY FROM THE TREE HOUSE

A Parachute Press Book

A MINSTREL® BOOK

Published by POCKET BOOKS
New York   London   Toronto   Sydney   Tokyo   Singapore

A MINSTREL PAPERBACK *Original*

A Minstrel Paperback published by
POCKET BOOKS, a division of Simon & Schuster Inc.
1230 Avenue of the Americas, New York, NY 10020

Copyright © 1996 by Parachute Press, Inc.

STAY AWAY FROM THE TREE HOUSE
WRITTEN BY LISA EISENBERG

All rights reserved, including the right to reproduce
this book or portions thereof in any form whatsoever.
For information address Pocket Books, 1230 Avenue
of the Americas, New York, NY 10020

ISBN: 0-671-52945-5

First Minstrel Books printing February 1996

10 9 8 7 6 5 4 3 2 1

FEAR STREET is a registered trademark of
Parachute Press, Inc.

A MINSTREL BOOK and colophon are registered trademarks
of Simon & Schuster Inc.

Cover art by Broeck Steadman

Printed in the U.S.A.

R·L·STINE'S
GHOSTS of FEAR STREET®

STAY AWAY FROM THE TREE HOUSE

I

For as long as I can remember, I've wanted to see a ghost. I don't think I'm asking a lot. I just want to meet one honest-to-goodness, terrifying, transparent, terrible ghost. Then I'll shut up about it.

It's really not fair that I haven't seen a ghost before this. Other kids around here have seen at least *one* spooky, hideous thing in their lives. But not me, Dylan Brown. No way. Even though I live on Fear Street, the scariest place in the world, my life has been the most boring, ordinary, totally ghost-free life in history.

But I had a feeling today was going to be different. Today was the day I was finally going to see a ghost.

Why?

Because it was definitely ghost weather today.

The morning had started out bright and sunny—a perfect spring day. But by the afternoon, heavy clouds rolled in and the sky turned dark and gloomy. Just the kind of weather ghosts like—don't you think?

Well, that's what I was thinking as I leaned back in Dad's squashy old green chair. I put the book I was reading in my lap and stared out the window. A strong wind was blowing now. And the tree branches in the front yard trembled.

Fear Street looks good and creepy today, I thought, pressing my nose against the window. *Perfect for finally meeting a creature from another world. So . . . where is it?*

It wasn't in my yard—that was obvious.

I stared left and right—into our neighbors' yards.

Nope. Nothing there.

Then I peered down the street.

And spotted something. A shadow. Darting out from behind a low bush. My heart raced—just a little.

Don't get your hopes up, I told myself. *It's probably Pokey, the neighbor's smelly old dog.*

I stared harder. It was still there. Hovering.

Maybe, just maybe, it isn't Pokey, I thought.

2

Maybe it's the ghost I've been waiting for my whole life.

Yes. This could be it. "Don't just sit here," I said out loud. "Go outside and check."

I closed my book—*The Book of Amazing All-True Ghost Stories*—and pictured myself marching across the street. I wasn't exactly sure how you were supposed to talk to a ghost. But I thought I'd say something like, "Come out now, Oh Unearthly One. Show yourself to me—Dylan S. Brown, fearless hunter of ghosts!"

A shadowy thing would ooze out from behind the bushes. As I stared at it, the thing would transform into a giant ghost-monster with glistening, knife-sharp teeth.

I wouldn't move an inch. No, I, Dylan S. Brown, ghost hunter would—

Bam!

Something behind me—something hard and icy—slammed down on my shoulder.

I leaped out of the chair, tripped over my own feet, and crashed to the floor.

"Get a grip, Dylan." My big brother stood over me, laughing his stupid head off. He held a Coke can in his hand—the cold can he had bashed into my shoulder. "You're turning into a bigger wimp every day."

I wanted to punch him in the knee. I had a great

3

shot at it from my spot on the floor. But if I did, Steve would probably tickle me.

He knows how much I hate being tickled. And he wouldn't stop until I promised to make his bed for a week.

So I didn't do anything—except sigh. Then I shoved myself up and said, "You surprised me, that's all." Boy, did that sound lame.

"Yeah, right," Steve replied. He took his baseball cap off his head and ran his fingers through his blond hair, smoothing it. Then he put the cap back on.

"I'll make you a deal. You do my paper route in the morning, and I won't tell everyone in school what a wimp you are."

I knew Steve wouldn't tell anyone. He could be a pain at home. But at school he always backed me up. "No way," I answered. "I'm not getting up at five in the morning to deliver your papers. And I'm not taking your turn doing the dishes or taking out the garbage either. So don't try to make another deal. Besides, I have better things to do."

"Oh, yeah. Like what?" Steve asked.

I pointed outside at the gloomy street. "Even you can see it's the perfect kind of day for finding a ghost."

"Oh, give me a break," Steve exclaimed. "You think *every* day is the perfect day for finding a

4

ghost! And you haven't found one yet. When are you going to admit that they don't exist?"

"When are you going to admit that they *do?*" I asked. "There are lots of ghosts on Fear Street. Just because you haven't seen one yet doesn't mean they're not there."

I could tell Steve wanted to interrupt me. I took a deep breath and rushed on. "Remember what Zack Pepper told me? His substitute teacher was really a ghost—and she almost pulled him back into her grave! Do you think that Zack is a liar?"

Steve shook his head. "No. Not a liar," he said. "Just crazy like you."

"Well, I believe him," I said. "Every single word."

My brother laughed. "That's the trouble with you, Dylan, my lad. You believe everything you hear. When you're my age, you'll know better."

I hate it when Steve calls me "my lad." I hate it more than I hate being tickled.

And I hate it when he says, "when you're my age." Steve's only one year older than I am. *One* year. He's in the sixth grade. I'm in the fifth. And he doesn't look older than me either. In fact, some people confuse us—we look that much alike. We both have blond hair, big green eyes, and tons of freckles.

"Whatever you say, Grandpa," I shot back.

Steve smiled one of his I'm-so-much-more-mature-than-you smiles and said, "Well, at least I'm old enough to know that there's no such thing as . . ."

Steve didn't finish his sentence.

He caught sight of something out the window. And now his eyes were locked on it.

He gasped.

"What?" I cried. "What is it?"

Steve swallowed hard. I could see the muscles in his neck pop out. "A-a ghost," he whispered, pointing outside with a shaky finger.

"Where?" I yelled.

I forgot I was angry and leaped forward so fast I smashed my face into the window. My nose felt as if someone had punched me. Hard.

But I didn't care. I shoved Steve aside so I could look for the ghost.

Then I heard a horrible sound.

A truly horrible sound.

Steve. Laughing.

"It's—it's—Pokey the dog," he stuttered. "The most hideous pooch to haunt Fear Street. I guess I made a little mistake," Steve said with a mean laugh.

I flopped down into the green chair and grabbed my book. "Someday I'm going to see a real ghost," I informed Steve. "And when I do, I won't even bother telling you about it."

"I'm really hurt," Steve wailed in a high little voice. Then he gave a loud sniffle.

I opened the book and pretended to read. Maybe Steve would take the hint and leave. He didn't.

"*You* would never see a ghost even if they did exist—which they don't," he continued. "Nothing exciting ever happens to *you*. And, if by some miracle you did see a ghost, you'd probably turn around and—"

BOOOOOM!

A thundering crash split the air.

The whole house rocked.

The lamp next to my chair toppled over and the lightbulb shattered, plunging us into darkness.

"St-Steve," I croaked. "Wh-what was that?"

2

"It-it came from the backyard," Steve whispered. His voice trembled slightly.

"Let's go see."

We tore through the house and out the back door. I jumped down the steps and almost landed right on top of my dad.

"Hi, guys," Dad called. "Guess you heard the crash." He put down the chain saw he was carrying.

"Crash? What crash?" Steve said, back to sounding like his usual obnoxious self.

"We heard it, Dad. What happened?" I asked.

Dad waved his hand toward the right side of the yard. A huge tree lay stretched out on the grass. It covered almost half our lawn.

"It's time to start clearing out the trees, boys," he explained, "if we want to get our pool in before summer."

"It looks like you almost cleared out the house, Dad," Steve joked.

For once I agreed with Steve. The top branches of the tree brushed against the house. If the tree had been a little bit taller, it would have slammed through the roof.

Dad wiped a bead of sweat from his face with a rag and laughed so hard his whole body shook up and down.

"Ha-ha. That's a good one, Steve. Ha-ho-ho!"

I rolled my eyes in disgust. My father always acts like Steve is a laugh riot. He never even understands my jokes.

Dad and Steve looked at the fallen tree as if they were scientists studying a moon rock.

"I guess I must have figured out the angle wrong on that one somehow," Dad said.

Steve shook his head as if he really had an opinion about the correct angle. Sometimes my brother just makes me sick.

I wandered over to the gap in the woods left by the huge tree. I could see into a part of the Fear Street woods I'd never been in. And way in the distance I saw something amazing.

"Steve," I yelled. "Steve, you are absolutely not

going to believe what's out there." Steve didn't look up.

"Steve!" I hollered. "Come on! Look! I think I see a tree house."

"Where?" Steve actually sounded a little interested.

"There, way deep in the woods. You can just see the top of it." I pointed straight ahead into the deep woods.

"Oh, yeah, I see what you mean," Steve admitted. "It might be a tree house—but how come we never saw it before?"

"I don't know, the branches of the other trees must have hidden it. Come on, let's go look for it."

Steve yawned. "I think I'll go inside and watch some TV," he said. "Tell me if you find it."

Is my brother the laziest person in the world, or what? "No way!" I answered. "I'm going to find the tree house. And I'm claiming it for myself!"

"Okay, okay," Steve said quickly. "I'll come with you. Just to make sure you don't get lost."

I knew that would get him. Steve can't stand it if I have something he doesn't.

"Don't go too far, guys," Dad warned. "It's almost dinnertime. I'm making my rigatoni with spicy meatballs tonight. It has to be served as soon as it's ready, or else it tastes like glue."

"Sure, Dad," I answered. Then I plunged into the woods and trotted along the rocky, overgrown trail.

Steve followed behind me. Complaining. As usual. "This path is bumpy," he griped. "And it's freezing out here!"

"You're right," I admitted. "I wonder why it's so cold."

I noticed my breath making frosty little clouds in front of my face. It *is* chilly for April, I thought. And the air seems to be getting colder with every step we take.

Steve tripped over a rock and fell flat on his face. He flipped over and glared at the rip in the knee of his favorite jeans. "This path stinks!" he yelled. "I'm going back."

I grabbed his arm and hauled him to his feet. "Let's keep going for a little while longer," I begged.

I didn't understand it, but something seemed to be pulling me into the woods. I couldn't stop now.

"No! I'm out of here." Steve turned and started back to the house.

"Wait! I have a deal for you."

Steve spun around. He loves deals. "It better be good," he warned.

"I'll do your paper route tomorrow morning."

He shook his head. "Not good enough," he said. "But if you deliver my papers every morning it

11

rains from now until the end of the year, I'll stay out here five more minutes. That's it. Take it or leave it."

"Ten more minutes," I said.

Steve nodded. "It's a deal."

We followed the overgrown path around a sharp curve—and that's when I saw it.

I stopped short and Steve bashed into me.

"What's wrong with you?" he complained.

I didn't speak. I couldn't.

I pointed to the top of a huge black oak tree standing alone in a clearing. On one side of the tree, an enormous branch rose up like a huge twisted arm, reaching up into the dark sky. Between the branch and the trunk, I could just see the remains of a platform, and a jagged section of wall.

The tree house.

"It looks like somebody dropped a bomb on it or something," Steve observed.

I trotted halfway across the clearing. "Look there," I whispered, pointing to the trunk of the black oak. "It used to have two levels. See that ladder that starts near the ground? It leads to a platform below the other one."

I noticed that half of the bottom platform was charred black. And there were no branches on that side of the tree.

I closed my eyes for a second and tried to picture

the tree house with both levels rebuilt. "This is so cool," I whispered.

"Great. Come on. Your ten minutes are up," Steve said.

I walked to the oak. Then I stopped.

I froze in horror.

Someone—or something—was standing at the base of the tree.

Almost hidden in the shadows.

It was a dark, shadowy, formless *thing* and I could see its eyes. Its cold, dark eyes.

And they were staring straight at me.

3

I opened my mouth to call my brother's name. But no sounds came out. My lips were suddenly too stiff to form words.

I silently told my legs to walk forward, toward the shapeless *thing*.

I was terrified, but I had to know whether it was a ghost. I had to find out if it even existed, or whether I was just imagining it.

But I just couldn't make myself move!

I swallowed hard three times. At last I was able to croak out a few words. "Steve," I whispered, "do you see that?"

"What?" Steve's voice rang out in the woods.

"What did you say, Dylan? Why are you whispering like that? I can't hear a word you're saying."

His words sounded so loud in the eerie silence. "Don't you see that . . . that *thing* over there by the tree?" I asked again. But before I'd even finished my sentence, the black form melted away into the shadows.

"Give it a rest, Dylan," Steve said.

"But I saw it!" I insisted, squinting at the tree. "A big, black kind of blobby shape. It was looking right at me, and . . ."

"Dy-lan! Steve! Din-ner!" My father's booming voice carried through the cold, clammy air. But he sounded so far away. "On the doub-le!"

"Come on." Steve yanked my arm.

But I was frozen to the spot. Staring at the tree. Hoping I'd see the shadowy figure one more time.

"You stay here if you want," Steve muttered. "I'm going home to eat."

"Okay, okay," I mumbled. "But can we come back?"

"Yeah, sure. We can come back," Steve said. "Another time. Like maybe in a hundred years."

Steve started back on the bumpy path. I glanced at the tree house one last time. Everything remained still.

That's when I realized how totally quiet the woods were.

No sounds at all.

Not even the chirp of a single bird.

Weird. Definitely weird.

I slowly turned and followed my brother. *I'm coming back,* I promised myself. *No matter how creepy these woods are . . . I'm coming back. This could finally be my chance to meet a ghost!*

As we hurried home, I noticed something else about the woods that was strange. The farther we got from the tree house, the warmer I felt.

Didn't one of my ghost books talk about cold spots in haunted houses? I had to read up on all the signs of ghost appearances right away!

Steve led the way inside, telling Mom and Dad, "Dylan's seeing things again." He really does treat me like a baby.

In the bright light of the kitchen I could hardly believe I'd seen the shadowy ghost out in the woods. But I knew I had. And I couldn't stop thinking about it.

During dinner I dribbled Dad's tomato sauce down my shirt. And Mom had to ask me three times to pass the bread.

I could hear Steve snickering at me, but I didn't care. The second I was excused from the table, I ran upstairs to my bedroom. I had to start my ghost research.

Steve barged into the room a few minutes later

and dropped down on the bottom bunk of our bunk beds. Then he reached into his backpack, pulled out a book, and groaned.

I already knew what was coming.

"Dylan, my lad, I have—"

"A deal for you," I finished.

"This is a really good one," Steve protested. "You write my social studies report for me, and I'll take back any rainy Mondays, Wednesdays, and Fridays for delivering my newspapers."

I noticed this deal left me with four days a week, while Steve had three.

And he stuck me with the Sunday papers.

Everyone knows those are the heaviest.

"No deal. I'll take my chances with the rain." I reached over to my bookshelf, grabbed my copy of *The A–Z Ghost Encyclopedia,* and looked up cold spots.

The encyclopedia confirmed that cold was a sign of a haunted place.

I knew it!

"What then?" Steve asked. He still hadn't bothered to open his social studies book. "What kind of deal do you want to make?"

"How about I write the paper, and you help me rebuild the tree house?" I suggested. "That—or nothing," I quickly added. I've learned a few things from Steve.

"No *way* am I helping you rebuild that tree house," Steve answered. "That would take as long as writing a hundred papers. That place is a total wreck."

"But think how cool it could be." I sat down at my desk, grabbed a big sheet of paper, and started sketching. "A two-level tree house of our own—where no one would bother us."

"It wouldn't be worth the work," Steve mumbled.

I ignored him and kept drawing. Then I held up the sketch.

"Whoa!" Steve exclaimed. "Do you really think you could make that awesome pulley thing and rebuild the second floor?"

"Sure. But I would definitely need your help on it."

That wasn't quite true. Steve would probably drive me nuts the whole time. But if the shadowy thing really *was* a ghost—and if it came back—I wanted Steve to see it. So I could prove to him—finally—that ghosts were real!

"Come on, Steve," I continued. "It'll be a cool place to hang out. And nobody could bug us about doing our homework up there." I left my chair and glanced out the window to see if I could spot the tree house.

"Hmmmm," Steve thought a minute, brushing

his hair back under his baseball cap. "Okay, I'm in."

Do I know the right thing to say to my brother, or what?

"But you have to do more of the work," Steve added. "Because you're the one who really wants the tree house."

"You are so . . ." My voice trailed off.

"So what?" Steve asked.

I didn't answer him.

I was staring out the window. Right where I thought the tree house stood.

"Look!" I shouted. "Look! There! A light—out by the tree house."

"You're probably seeing things, as usual," Steve grumbled. He rolled off the bed and shuffled over to the window. He leaned close to the glass and cupped his hands around his eyes. "Hey! There *is* a light bouncing around out there."

"Why would someone be out in the woods at night?" I wondered out loud.

"That's a good question," Steve replied.

We stared out the window in silence. Watching the light bob and flicker.

Could it be the ghost? Maybe, I decided. But why would a ghost need light?

There was only one way to find out for sure. "Let's go and check it out," I said quietly.

To my amazement, Steve didn't argue or try to make a deal. He pulled a sweatshirt out of his middle drawer and yanked it over his head.

"This time, I'm not going to freeze to death," he announced. "Come on. What are you waiting for?" Steve grinned at me and slapped me a high five.

Every once in a while having a brother can be cool.

Steve turned on the radio before we left our room. "Better have some noise in here."

Steve was right—sometimes Mom and Dad get suspicious if we are *too* quiet. Dad claims it's because they're afraid we've killed each other. Ha-ha.

I followed Steve down the stairs. We both stepped over the third step. That's the one that creaks.

As we crept through the kitchen I snagged a flashlight from the junk drawer. We cut across the backyard and entered the woods. Then I flipped the flashlight on.

It didn't help much. We both tripped over rocks and roots. We'd only gone about three feet when Steve started asking the same question over and over again.

"Why?" he chanted. "Why, why, why? Why did I agree to do this?" With each step he took, he muttered, "Why?"

I wanted to tell him to shut up. But I didn't want to make him angry. I didn't want him to turn back.

When we had made it about halfway there, Steve changed his chant. He changed it to "Cold. Cold, cold, cold."

He was really getting annoying now. But I had to admit it—it was cold. I was shivering.

But that was a good sign!

Yes. Cold was definitely a good sign.

Because cold meant ghosts!

"Do you see anything?" Steve whispered in my ear.

"No—wait. Maybe." I stared hard at the big oak tree. "There!" I pointed. "I just saw a light on that side of the tree. Then it went out."

I dug my heels into the ground— planting them there firmly—so it would be harder to bolt, which is exactly what I wanted to do.

I cleared my throat.

"Who is there?" My voice squeaked.

The light flashed again.

Then it went out.

Swoosh, swoosh, swoosh.

"D-did you hear that?" I asked Steve. He nodded.

Something was moving in the dark.

Swoosh, swoosh, swoosh.

21

There it was again. Like ghostly feet sliding over the grass. Moving. Toward us.

I swung the flashlight around wildly. Trying to catch it in my beam.

Then I heard another sound. A voice. A laugh.

"Steve, did you hear that?" I whispered. "It laughed."

"Shine your light over there," Steve whispered back.

He sounded scared. I knew I was.

I swung my flashlight in that direction—and two humanlike forms walked toward us.

Girls.

Two girls squinting in the light and giggling.

Two totally alive girls.

4

I wanted a ghost. Or a werewolf. Or a vampire. Even a mummy.

But no. I found girls.

"Who are you?" Steve asked as we walked toward them. "What are you doing out here?"

"I'm Kate Drennan," one of the girls answered in a soft voice. "And this is my sister, Betsy."

Both girls had bright blue eyes and long black hair. The one named Kate had straight hair tied back in a ponytail. The other one had wavy hair with curls that tumbled all the way down her back.

I'd never seen either of them before—even though they looked as though they should be in my grade.

"We were just—" Kate began again. But before she could finish, Betsy cut her off.

"Why do you get to ask the questions?" she demanded. "We have as much right to be here as you do."

"Okay, okay," I started to apologize. "It's just that I've never seen you around here before. Do you go to Shadyside Middle School?"

"No," Kate started to answer.

"We're on spring break," Betsy interrupted. "We go to school in Vermont. We don't know many kids in Shadyside, so it gets pretty boring."

"That's why we sneaked out tonight," Kate added. "We were bored. There was nothing on TV. Nothing to do."

"We sneaked out, too," I admitted.

Kate—the nicer one—smiled. And Betsy—the bossy one—seemed to relax a little.

"At least you get a vacation," Steve added. "We don't have one until school lets out for the summer."

"We should head back," Betsy said. "Our parents might check up on us or something."

"Us, too. We'll probably see you around," I volunteered. "We'll be out here a lot—we're going to rebuild that tree house."

I shone the flashlight up into the branches of the big, dark oak. Both girls glanced up. Then I noticed

Kate's expression. She looked scared. Really scared.

Betsy glared at me. "What did you say?" she asked.

"I said we're going to rebuild that old tree house."

"That's what I thought you said," Betsy replied. "But you can't."

"Why can't we?" Steve demanded.

"No one can," Betsy insisted.

Kate began chewing nervously on the end of her ponytail. "You can't rebuild the tree house," she said. "You can't because . . . because . . ."

"Because of the secret about it," Betsy finished for her sister.

"The secret?" I asked. "What secret?"

5

A tree house with a secret! Is this cool or what?

"We can't tell you. Everyone knows about this old tree house," Betsy snapped.

Then she narrowed her eyes. "But I *will* tell you this—if you don't want to get hurt . . . you'll stay away from the tree house!"

"They're just trying to scare us," Steve replied. "But it's not going to work. Right?"

"Right," I replied, not feeling as convinced as I sounded.

"Well, I, uh, really think you should listen to Betsy," Kate whispered. "Because we, um, we heard some kids tried to fix up the tree house and they . . ."

"What happened to them?" These girls were driving me crazy. "Did they die? What happened?"

Betsy shook her sister's shoulder, interrupting her for the millionth time. "Come on. Let's go. They don't need to hear that old story," she snapped. "If they're smart, they'll just stay away."

"Why? Why should we stay away?" I asked. Then I remembered what I had read about ghosts and cold spots. "Wow!" I said. "Is the tree house haunted?"

"Come on, Kate," Betsy ordered. "These guys are hopeless."

Kate gave a sort of half smile. "We do have to go," she said. "Our mom will freak if she can't find us."

"Wait!" I protested. "Just tell us some more about the tree house. Please!"

I thought Kate was about to say something, but Betsy didn't give her a chance. "I said come *on,*" she grumbled, tugging her sister across the clearing.

"Bye," Kate called over her shoulder.

As they stepped onto the path, Betsy stopped and called back, "Remember, you have been warned. Now if anything bad happens to you, it will be your own fault!"

The next day at school, I couldn't concentrate. Betsy's warning kept echoing in my head. What did it mean? What was the big secret about the tree house?

It must be haunted, I decided. That had to be it. At least I hoped so.

I spent the last part of the day—the part when we were supposed to be doing math—drawing tree house plans on the cover of my notebook.

In some of the plans, I sketched a shadowy figure sitting on the end of a branch. I made it shadowy because I didn't know what a ghost really looked like. Not yet, anyway.

As soon as the last bell rang, I raced home. I headed straight into the garage and loaded up two big cardboard boxes with nails, old boards, and lots of tools.

That was the easy part.

Next came the hard part—Steve. I found him lying on the couch, watching TV, and munching Cheese Curlies.

"Come on," I said. "We have to start before it gets too dark out there."

Steve's eyes remained glued to the screen. "Let's wait till Saturday," he answered. "I want to watch the rest of this show."

I glanced at the TV. "You've seen that cartoon at least one hundred times!" I snatched the remote from his hand and clicked off the TV. "We had a deal."

"Our deal didn't say *when* I had to help," Steve answered. "What's the big rush, anyway?"

"I think the tree house is haunted! I think someone died up there! And I did see something in the shadows."

"Dylan," Steve said, shaking his head, "the only thing that died is your brain."

"I can *prove* to you that ghosts are real," I replied. "Just think about it—this is the perfect chance for us to settle our argument about ghosts. If the tree house is haunted, I know I can prove it."

Steve shoved himself up from the sofa.

"All right, Dylan, my lad. But if we don't see a ghost before we finish the tree house, you have to admit I was right and you were wrong."

"Sure. Let's go."

"And you have to stop talking about ghosts, reading about ghosts, watching movies about ghosts—even thinking about ghosts. Deal?" Steve asked.

"Deal," I agreed.

We headed to the garage to pick up the supplies. Steve chose the lightest box, of course.

We cut across the backyard, and I led the way into the woods. "Wow!" Steve cried as he stumbled along behind me. "The woods are even colder than last night. From now on, I'm wearing my winter parka when we come out here."

"It's because of the ghost," I informed him. "Haunted places usually have a colder temperature."

"Give me a break!" Steve shouted. "It's cold because of all the trees. The sunlight can't get through the branches."

After that we trudged along without talking. My box felt heavier with every step. I thought about turning around and asking Steve to trade. But I didn't want to start another argument.

I stopped when the path reached the clearing.

I scanned the shadows around the oak tree.

Nothing there.

I dumped my cardboard box on the ground. I turned to Steve—and couldn't believe what I saw. "Where's yours?" I demanded.

"Where's my what?" Steve asked, smiling.

"Your *box.*"

Steve took off his baseball cap, smoothed his hair, and stuck the cap back on. "I left it at the edge of the backyard. We couldn't possibly use all that junk in one day," Steve explained.

"That was not our deal!" I yelled. "Our deal was that you help. Watching me carry a box does not count as help. And neither does leaving our stuff behind!"

"Okay, okay. I'll get the box," Steve muttered.

I watched Steve disappear down the path—and

realized what a big mistake I had made. I'd be lucky if Steve returned—with or without the box.

In fact, I knew exactly what Steve would do. He would decide he needed a glass of water. No, a glass of water and some more Cheese Curlies—to build up his strength. And since he couldn't eat and carry the box at the same time, he'd watch a few cartoons until he finished the Curlies. And by then, it would be time for me to go home.

Well, I didn't need Steve, anyway. I really didn't expect him to do much work. I just wanted him along because the woods were kind of creepy. Which is exactly what I started thinking as I opened the carton.

It was quiet here. Way too quiet.

And dark. Steve was right about the branches. They blocked out all the sunlight.

I glanced up at the tree house and felt a shiver race up and down my spine. *You wanted to see a ghost,* I told myself. *And now's your chance.*

I forced myself to march over to the tree. I tested the first rung of the ladder nailed onto the trunk. A little wobbly, but okay, I decided.

I stepped on the rung. It held me—no problem. I tugged on the second rung before I climbed up—it felt okay, too. Only three more rungs to go.

I stared up at the tree house again. An icy breeze swept over me and my knees began to shake.

Take a deep breath, I told myself. *Don't wimp out now.*

I stepped up to the next rung.

And that's when I heard the sound.

A sickening *crack.*

My feet flew out from under me as the third rung snapped off the trunk.

I flung my arms around the tree. I kicked my legs wildly, searching for a foothold. I tried to pull myself up to the fourth rung.

My heart pounded in my chest until my feet found it. Then I clung there for a few minutes. Hugging the tree trunk tightly, trying to catch my breath.

A cold gust of wind blew. My teeth began to chatter.

I inhaled deeply. "Okay, just one more rung to go," I said out loud. But I couldn't move. I remained frozen to the spot.

Then I pictured myself talking to Steve after I'd proven that ghosts exist. "Steve, my lad," I would say, "don't feel stupid. Even though you are a year older, no one expects you to be right about everything."

That gave me the courage to go on.

I made my way to the top rung. I peered underneath the tree house and studied the platform. Half of it was badly damaged. The boards were charred black. But the other half appeared solid enough. I banged on the boards with my fist a few times just to make sure.

Then I pulled myself through the open trapdoor—and felt something touch my face. Something soft. Something airy. Something light.

I screamed.

I found the ghost!

6

I leaped back. But the ghost wrapped itself around me. It covered my face. I couldn't breathe.

"Get away from me! Get away from me!" I screamed. My arms flailed as I tried to fight it off.

Its touch was sticky. It felt like—spiderwebs.

Spiderwebs.

I wasn't battling a ghost. I was fighting spiderwebs.

I guess that should have made me feel better, but it didn't. Because the more I fought, the more tangled up I got.

I shook my hands, but the webs wouldn't come off. And my fingers started to burn and itch.

I tried to brush the webs out of my face. I could

feel them clinging to my eyelashes. They were in my ears. My nostrils. My mouth.

"Get off! Get off!" I screamed as I clawed at my face.

They pressed in tighter.

They were suffocating me.

I couldn't breathe.

I stumbled around the tree house until I found the trapdoor. Then I lowered myself through the hole. I didn't bother feeling around for the rungs. I slid all the way down the tree trunk.

When I reached the ground, Steve was standing there. "Help me get these things off!" I yelled. "They're all over me. I almost choked to death!"

Steve pulled off his jacket and brushed the webs off with it. I grabbed it and wiped my face.

"Are you okay?" Steve asked.

I nodded.

"Then give me back my jacket."

I threw it at him. He shook it out and pulled it over his head.

Even though the webs were gone, I couldn't stop scratching.

"There weren't *that* many," Steve commented as he watched me.

"I couldn't breathe!" I protested.

"You just scared yourself," he said. "You're so

convinced there's a ghost up there that you freaked."

"I almost died!" What did Steve know? He wasn't the one in the tree house.

"Hey! Maybe that's what that weird girl meant when she said the tree house was dangerous," Steve said.

"What? What do you mean?"

"Killer cobwebs," he replied.

"That's funny, Steve. Real funny." I closed up the carton with our tools and shoved it up against the tree. "We'll leave it here until tomorrow—"

When you go up to the tree house first, I added to myself. *And you're the one smothered in itchy, burning spiderwebs. Then we'll see how you like it, Steve. Then we'll see.*

The next morning was Saturday. Finally! A whole day to work on the tree house. I got up early and waited for Steve on the porch. I checked my watch. Seven A.M. Steve would be here any minute.

The minute I sat down on the front steps, Steve rounded the corner on his bicycle. He rode up and dumped his bike on the lawn.

"Ready?" I asked him, jumping up.

"Yep. Ready," he replied. He plowed past me and headed for the door. "Ready to go back to bed."

"Hey!" I cried, running to the door and bracing

both arms against the frame to block his way. "You agreed to work all day on the tree house."

"I'm going back to sleep. I'll help you when I get up." He shoved me aside.

"Doughnuts," I said just as he turned the knob. "Double-dipped chocolate doughnuts."

"You've got doughnuts?" Steve asked.

"In my backpack. Mom drove me down to the Donut Hole."

"Hand them over," Steve ordered. "Mom didn't buy them just for you." He took a few steps toward me. Then he lunged for my backpack.

"Mom didn't buy them," I said, leaping back. "*I* did. With my own money. And I'm taking them out to the tree house."

I pushed past Steve and ran around the house. I could hear his feet pounding right behind me.

Halfway to the clearing, Steve caught up to me and yanked my backpack off. He pawed through it and grabbed a doughnut with each hand.

"You'll never be able to outrun me, Dylan, my lad," Steve declared. He took a big bite of one doughnut. Then he followed me down the path.

Do I know my brother, or what?

When we reached the clearing, I handed Steve another doughnut and took one for myself. "It's your turn to deal with the spiderwebs today," I announced.

I pulled an old house painter's mask out of my backpack and tossed it to Steve. "Wear this. At least it will keep the webs out of your nose and mouth."

"I don't need it," he said, tossing it aside. Then he began climbing up the tree.

I stared up and watched him climb. Even though it was a bright sunny morning, the tree house was cloaked in darkness. A breeze rustled the leaves. A cold breeze.

Steve entered the tree house through the trapdoor. "Oh, no!" he cried out.

"What?" I yelled. "Is it the ghost?"

"No, you idiot. I forgot to take the hammer," he replied, laughing. "Hand it up to me. The one with the big claw on the end. I'll need to pry some of these boards up. And give me some new boards, too, while you're at it."

No ghosts. No spiderwebs.

I wasn't sure what disappointed me more. I handed Steve the stuff he needed. Then I started working on a new ladder. I grabbed a saw from one of the cardboard boxes and found some small pieces of wood that I could cut into rungs.

As I sawed, I kept thinking about the spiderwebs. Maybe Steve was right. Maybe I just panicked yesterday.

But maybe, I thought, *just maybe, the ghost*

wrapped all those webs around my head. One of my books said some ghosts would do anything to keep humans away.

I yanked off the old rungs and began hammering the new ones into place. I was rummaging through the carton to find some nails when I realized I didn't hear Steve hammering anymore.

"Steve? How's it going up there?" I called.

No answer.

He better not be sleeping, I thought. *Not after I spent my allowance on his favorite doughnuts.*

"Steve?"

No reply.

"I'd better wake him up," I said, grumbling. I climbed up the first two rungs of the ladder and peered up.

And that's when I saw it.

The hammer.

With the big black claw at one end.

Plunging down.

Plunging straight for my face.

7

I let go of the tree and hurled myself to the ground.

Thwack! The hammer landed inches away from my nose.

"Steve!" I yelled. "You almost killed me with that hammer."

I shoved myself to my feet. My jeans were torn and my knee throbbed.

"Don't pretend you aren't up there," I bellowed. Still no answer.

I scrambled up the rungs and poked my head through the trapdoor. No Steve.

"Now what are you screaming about, Dylan, my lad?" Steve stood halfway across the clearing, holding a bag of Cheese Curlies.

"How—how did you get over there?"

"I went back to the house for these," he said, holding up the orange bag. "You were so busy sawing you didn't notice." He grinned. "Want some?"

"No, I don't want some," I shouted. "Your hammer almost hit me in the head. Why did you leave it near the trapdoor?" I asked.

"I didn't," Steve replied. "I left it in the middle of the platform."

"You did not," I screamed.

"Did, too," Steve screamed back.

"Hey, is something wrong?" It was that girl Betsy. She and her sister, Kate, stepped out from behind the tree.

"We heard yelling," Kate said. "We thought someone was hurt." She tugged on the end of her ponytail.

"Someone *was* almost hurt." I glared at Steve. "Me. That thing came flying straight at me," I said, pointing to the hammer on the ground. "It could have smashed my head open."

"What thing?" Kate asked. Her eyes showed real concern—fear, even.

"Steve's hammer. He left it on the edge and it fell and nearly killed me." I was practically shouting.

"That's just what happened the last time," Betsy said.

Then they both nodded.

"What happened? What last time?" Now Steve was shouting.

"You must have made it very angry," Betsy said.

"I made the hammer angry? Are you crazy?" I was practically yelling at them. Why did they always have to talk in riddles?

"Not the hammer," Kate whispered. *"It."*

"Who is *it?"* I demanded.

"There is no *it,"* Steve cut in. "Get real, Dylan. The wind probably blew the hammer down. Or a squirrel knocked it over."

"Believe whatever you want." Betsy smirked. "But we warned you. We warned you not to work on the tree house."

I turned toward Kate. She was chewing the end of her ponytail now.

"You made it angry," Betsy said again. "It's not a good idea to make a ghost angry."

8

"**T**ell me. Tell me about the ghost," I begged.

"I guess we have to tell them." Betsy turned toward her sister. "If we don't, they'll never finish the tree house—alive."

The four of us sat down in a circle. Betsy's eyes darted around the clearing. "I don't know if it's safe to tell this—especially so close to where it happened."

"Please—" I started.

Betsy held up her hand, signaling me to shut up. Then she began the story.

"A long time ago three kids around our age built the tree house. They drew hundreds of pictures of it first—until they agreed on how it should look.

They wanted it to be the most perfect tree house ever. Then they spent weeks and weeks up there. Hammering. Sawing. Making sure everything fit just right."

"Ooooh, I'm starting to get scared already," Steve said, rolling his eyes.

"Ignore him," I told Betsy.

"The night the tree house was finished, the kids decided to sleep in it. They brought some food and their sleeping bags. And they stayed up late— telling ghost stories.

"Suddenly, a thunderstorm rolled in. Streaks of lightning cut through the sky. But the kids weren't scared. They thought it was cool to be there. A great night for ghost stories."

I nodded. I know how much I like to read my ghost books when it's cold and gray. Ghost weather.

"Then a strong wind picked up. The branches beneath the tree house began to sway. And the tree house creaked and groaned. A blast of thunder made the tree shake. They all screamed in terror.

"They talked about going home. But the rain was coming down hard now. They decided to wait out the storm. Strong storms like these never lasted long, they thought.

"And then it happened.

"A lightning bolt shattered the clouds. It sliced

44

through the heavy treetops and pierced the tree house.

"The tree house burst into flames."

Betsy swallowed hard.

Lightning. That made sense. I remembered the charred black boards in the lower platform.

"The kids were up on the top platform," Betsy continued. "They couldn't escape. The horrible flames leaped up in front of them. Behind them.

"Thick black smoke billowed everywhere.

"They cried out for help—but it was too late."

"Some people say you can still hear their terrifying screams on rainy nights," Kate whispered.

I stared over at the tree house. I pictured it in flames. I imagined the cries The horrible cries for help. I shuddered.

"So that's it?" Steve asked. "That's why we shouldn't build the tree house? We're not dumb enough to stay in a tree house in a thunderstorm."

"That's not why," I said. I understood what Betsy was trying to tell us. "The tree house is haunted now, right? It's haunted by the ghosts of the kids."

Betsy nodded. Then she went on.

"Many years after the accident, some kids tried to rebuild the tree house. But they didn't have time to finish it. . . ."

45

"What happened to them?" I whispered. I could feel my heart pounding in my chest as Betsy continued.

"No one knows the whole story. At first, little things went wrong. One of the boys fell off the ladder—a rung broke."

"Big deal," Steve interrupted. "The wood was probably old—so it broke."

Betsy continued. "But it wasn't an old rung—it was one of the new ones they had just fixed. Another kid came down with a strange fever. It turned out he had like a million spider bites."

Spider bites.

I could feel the spiderwebs on my face as she talked.

"Then things got really strange. No matter how hard they worked—the tree house was never finished. Boards that were hammered in one day were found on the ground the next day.

"Finally the kids realized the tree house was haunted. They stopped working on it—all except for one kid. I think his name was Duncan."

"What happened to Duncan?" Steve asked.

"He kept working on the tree house. Until . . . until one day his brother found him. He was lying under the tree house. A hammer had fallen and knocked him out."

"Was he dead?" I managed to croak.

"No one knows," Kate said. "His family moved away after that. And no one has dared to go near the tree house since then."

I glanced around the woods. Nothing moved. Everything was silent. So silent I could hear Kate's soft breathing across from me.

"Now you know why you can't work on the tree house," Kate said. "We probably shouldn't even be in this clearing. We're too close. Much too close."

"You're right," Betsy said. "Let's get out of here. This place is giving me the creeps."

"Are you going?" Kate asked.

I didn't answer. There were too many thoughts racing around in my brain. The webs . . . The hammer . . . That kid Duncan . . . The haunted tree house . . .

"We've got some stuff to do," I finally answered. "We'll see you around."

Betsy gave me a long, hard stare. "I don't think you're going to be around much longer," she said. "Not if you stay here."

Then she grabbed Kate's arm and they ran across the clearing and disappeared into the woods.

"Those girls are seriously weird," Steve said. "Even weirder than you, Dylan. They're really scared some ghost is going to swoop down and grab them."

"You don't think that story is true?" I asked.

47

"Of course not," Steve shot back. "Ghosts don't exist, Dylan, my lad. Trust me. I'm older. I know more than you do."

Yeah, right, I thought. "Then how did that story get started? And what happened to the hammer in the middle of the platform? How come it fell on me?"

Steve groaned.

"I'll tell you how come that hammer fell," I said to Steve. "The ghost threw it at me—as a warning!"

9

I managed to trick, bargain, or bribe Steve into working on the tree house every day until Friday. On Fridays Steve has band practice. He smashes cymbals together once or twice during a concert—then he brags about what a great musician he is.

So I had to go out to the tree house alone. *This probably isn't such a good idea,* I thought as I walked through the woods. The ghost Kate and Betsy had described didn't exactly sound friendly. But if there was a ghost out there, I wanted to see it, I decided. No matter what.

I thought about the girls' story—the broken rung on the ladder. The spider bites. The hammer.

The hammer. A shiver ran through me. I sure

was luckier than that boy Duncan. But would my luck hold out?

The clearing was just up ahead.

I walked a few steps into it and stopped.

"Oh, no!" I groaned.

All our boards and nails—all of them—had been destroyed.

They lay scattered everywhere—all over the clearing, between the trees—everywhere. I even spotted some boards on the ground deep in the forest.

They were all bent and twisted. Deformed.

I swallowed hard and stared up at the dark windows of the tree house. Nothing moved inside.

I slowly crossed the clearing.

I glanced up at the tree house before each step.

I was terrified—terrified that the ghost was getting ready to swoop down on me.

I reached the base of the old oak and stood there. Waiting. Waiting for something to happen.

Nothing did.

So I began cleaning up the mess, nervously checking over my shoulder every few minutes.

It would take me hours to find all the nails and clean up this mess. Now I was more angry than scared.

"It's going to take more than this to stop me!" I yelled out. "I'm not like those other kids!"

When I stopped screaming the woods felt quieter than ever. Spookier.

That's right, Dylan, I thought. *Invite the ghost to come out and pound you. Very smart.*

I glanced around. Nothing moved.

I grabbed one of the cardboard boxes and began tossing nails into it. Nails that I had straightened out. This was going to take forever.

At this moment the only one I hated more than the ghost was Steve. How come he always manages to be busy when I need him the most?

After I had gathered up all the nails I could find, I began collecting the boards. I stacked up the ones in the clearing first. Then I gathered the others that had been tossed in the woods.

As I hauled the last one back to the clearing, I peered up at the tree house—and spotted something high on the trunk.

I wasn't sure what it was. I walked a few steps closer and squinted.

Claw marks.

It looked like claw marks.

Huge, black claw marks.

I'd never seen an animal with claws big enough to make those marks. And I wasn't even sure a big animal could get way up there.

But there was one thing I *was* sure about—those marks weren't there yesterday.

I moved closer to the tree and stared hard. That's when I realized I wasn't staring at claw marks.

I was looking at something worse. Much worse.

They were letters. Letters burned into the trunk of the tree.

My heart pounded as I spelled out the message. S-T-A-Y-A-W-A-Y.

Stay away!

10

~~~

"**G**et real, Dylan," Steve said. "For the hundredth time, there are no ghosts. Not here. Not in the tree house. Not anywhere."

"What about the letters?" I spat back.

"Well, Dylan, my lad. I have a theory about those letters. I think you put them there," he said, "to make me believe in ghosts. It was a nice try—but it's not going to work."

I wanted to strangle Steve.

But I made a suggestion instead.

"We can settle our ghost argument once and for all tonight," I told him.

"Why? What happens tonight?" he asked.

"Tonight we are going to sleep out in the woods. And we are going to finally meet a ghost."

It took the usual arguments before Steve agreed to sleep outside with me that night.

"You want me to camp out in the freezing cold—without any TV? Are you crazy?" he hollered.

"You're not afraid, are you?" I challenged.

"How can I be afraid of something that doesn't exist?" Steve snapped. "You're the one who's always getting spooked. I'm just not doing it—that's all."

"Do you still have that book report to write for your English class?" I asked.

And that was the end of that. Steve and I were going to sleep out.

"The deal was that I sleep out with you tonight," Steve said as he squirmed his way into his sleeping bag. "That means I sleep. You watch."

"How am I going to prove ghosts exist if I can't wake you up when one appears?" I argued.

"It's not going to happen, Dylan," he answered. He closed his eyes and rolled over on his side. "But if it does, if by some miracle you're right and I'm wrong and you find a ghost—you can wake me up. But you'd better be absolutely sure it's a ghost. Or I'll pound you."

54

My brother is such an idiot, I thought. But it's better to be out in the woods with an idiot than with no one at all.

I didn't plan to sleep. So I sat cross-legged on my sleeping bag, with my flashlight, camera, and tape recorder all ready to go.

I also had a thermometer so I'd know how cold the ghost made the air. And a compass—to study its effect on the earth's magnetic field.

I even put a plate of cookies and crackers and Cheese Curlies at the bottom of the oak tree. I'd always wondered if ghosts ate. None of my books mentioned food. But I wanted to be prepared for anything.

I was ready.

I pressed the record button on the tape recorder. "Testing one, two. Testing. This is Dylan S. Brown," I whispered into it. It is Friday, April 21st, 10:38 P.M. My assistant, Steve Brown, and I successfully sneaked out of the house.

"We have set up a base camp in the Fear Street Woods, near the clearing next to the tree house. I hope the trees will hide us from the ghost. I want to observe it before I decide to make contact. It is too dark to photograph the words I discovered burned into the tree trunk. I will document them tomorrow."

Steve gave a little half-snort, half-snore. "My assistant has fallen asleep," I continued. "More later." I clicked off the tape recorder.

I raised my binoculars and studied the tree house.

No lights.

No movement.

Nothing staring back at me.

I let the binoculars fall back around my neck.

Then I heard a rustling sound. Not very loud—but coming from the direction of the tree house.

Something was definitely out there.

I thought about waking Steve up. But I didn't. I wasn't sure yet if it was the ghost. And if it wasn't, he'd kill me.

I picked up my binoculars and pressed them to my face.

I peered into the darkness.

I couldn't see a thing.

Should I turn on my flashlight? I wanted to, but if I did whatever was out there would see me. And I didn't want to scare it off.

I listened hard. There it was again. That same rustling sound. Even though I was wearing my blue winter parka, I shivered. The air around me felt colder now.

I checked the thermometer. Five degrees cooler than before. I knew it!

My pulse began to race. Chills ran up and down my spine.

I should be taping this, I thought. With a shaky hand I punched on the record button.

Should I wake Steve up now?

No. Not yet. I needed more proof.

The noise again. Louder this time.

Part of me wanted to duck down into my sleeping bag and zip it over my head. But I couldn't. I had to get closer. I had to see my ghost.

I picked up the flashlight and crawled away from my sleeping bag. I dodged behind the closest tree. The noise continued. The ghost didn't spot me.

I stayed low to the ground—on my hands and knees.

Crawling from tree to tree.

Crawling closer to the old oak.

My heart pounded so hard I thought it would burst out of my chest.

But now I was there. Behind a large rock right next to the old oak.

I peeked out from behind my hiding spot. Too dark. I still couldn't see anything. But I could hear it.

I steadied my flashlight in my trembling hand. I held it straight out in front of me. I flipped it on.

Two cold, dark eyes were caught in its beam.

A cat.

A gray cat eating Cheese Curlies.

I let out the longest sigh of my life.

Beads of sweat dripped from my forehead. I sank back against the tree and wiped them off.

Creak.

I jerked my head back toward the old oak.

Creak.

The cat darted into the woods.

Creak.

I recognized that sound—the sound of someone walking on the old wooden boards of the tree house.

Creak. Creak.

This is it, I thought. This is really it. I stood up and inched closer to the tree house.

I held my breath. I was afraid to breathe. Afraid the ghost would hear me.

I stood a foot away from the tree house. I squinted up into the darkness.

One of the boards on the wall of the tree house moved . . . as if someone up there was shaking it.

I heard the sound of nails—nails squealing as they were pried loose.

Then *pop!* I saw the board flip up. And suddenly, as I watched, it came hurtling through the air.

"Steve!" I shrieked. "Steve! It's the ghost. It's the ghost. It's tearing apart our tree house!"

CRASH!

The board hit the ground a few feet from me.

Ping ping ping.

Nails flew through the air, bouncing off the branches of the surrounding trees.

I raced over to Steve. I shook him hard. "Get up!" I screamed. "Get up!"

"What?" he muttered, rubbing his eyes.

Creak!

"Run!" I yelled. "Run! It's coming after us."

Another board came soaring out of the tree house.

THUD!

It hit the ground right next to my sleeping bag.

59

I tore down the path. Steve was right behind me. We had to get home before the ghost grabbed us.

I couldn't see where I was going. But I didn't slow down.

A tree branch slashed across my face. A trickle of blood dripped down my cheek. I kept running. My lungs burned. I gasped for air.

My aching legs cried out for me to stop. But I couldn't stop. Not now.

I burst into the backyard.

Did Steve make it?

I spun around to check.

He almost ran right into me. "What did you—" he began.

Then his mouth dropped open. He was staring at something over my shoulder. "Oh, no," he whispered.

Then I felt it. Something big, cold, and clammy clutching the back of my shirt.

It grabbed the back of my neck and pulled me across the wet grass!

12

My knees buckled underneath me. I began to sink to the ground.

"Let me go!" I screamed. "I promise I'll stay away from your tree house!" But the ghost raised me up.

"What are you doing out here?"

Dad.

"We were camping out to catch a ghost," I explained in a rush. "It came after us. We almost didn't get away in time."

"What's going on out there?" Mom stood under the back door light. I could see her tighten the belt on her old pink robe.

"In the house," Dad ordered us. "Dylan and

Steve were hunting ghosts in the woods," he explained to Mom.

She held the door open for us. "How could you go out this late at night?" she asked, really angry.

"Why were you running?" Dad asked. "What happened?"

"Nothing happened," Steve muttered. He sounded totally calm.

"Nothing happened?" I squeaked. "The ghost—"

"It's late," Dad interrupted. "You two get to bed. We'll discuss this in the morning."

Steve and I slunk up the stairs to our room. "What do you mean nothing happened?" I demanded the second Steve shut the door behind us.

"I mean nothing happened," Steve answered. "You got scared and ran back here. I came after you."

"Oh, right!" I cried. "You were scared, too."

"No, I wasn't," Steve replied. "There was nothing to be scared of."

"What about the board? You saw the board crash to the ground."

"Oh, that's a really big deal," Steve said, laughing. "A board from an old wrecked tree house fell down. A tree house that's falling apart. What a shock!"

"It wasn't just one board," I protested. "And it

didn't just come loose. The ghost pried it loose. It's just like what happened to the kids Betsy told us about. The ghost doesn't want us to finish the tree house—so he's taking it apart."

"Listen to me," Steve replied. "I'm older. I know more than you do. And there are no such things as ghosts, Dylan. No ghosts! No ghosts!"

"You don't know that for sure."

Steve jumped off his bed. He pulled a pair of high-tops out of the closet and pulled them on. "You are driving me insane. We're going back to the tree house. Right now."

"What?"

"You heard me." Steve pulled on a red sweatshirt over the one he already wore. "We're settling this ghost thing tonight. We're going to check out the tree house. And you're going to admit that there's no such things as ghosts."

Steve opened our door. "Come on," he whispered.

I didn't move.

I didn't need any more proof of ghosts. And I didn't care what Steve thought.

I had seen enough.

Ghosts were real.

And scary.

"Dylan! Let's go."

I shook my head no.

"Aha! So you admit it!" he cried.

Half of me wanted to jump in bed and never come out. The other half wanted to strangle Steve.

I had no choice. I crept down the stairs after my brother.

"Ssstop," Steve hissed when we were almost to the kitchen door. "Mom and Dad are in there."

We froze. "I'm worried about Dylan," Mom said. "All he talks about is ghosts. He has no other interests."

"You should have seen him in the backyard. He looked terrified. Maybe tonight was enough to convince him to give up," Dad replied.

"I hope so," Mom answered. "Why don't you go up and check on them."

"Go!" Steve whispered. He pushed me toward the stairs.

We flew up to our room. Steve eased our door shut. I scrambled into the top bunk and pulled up the covers.

I heard Dad coming up the stairs. Oh, no! We left the light on. Too late to do anything about it.

I squeezed my eyes shut and tried to breathe deeply.

Our door opened. "Must be even more scared than I thought," Dad muttered. "They left the light on."

64

That's when I realized my right foot was sticking out of the covers.

And I still had my shoes on. If Dad noticed my sneaker, it was over.

Dad stood in the doorway for a long moment. Should I pull my foot in? Or would that draw attention to it?

I knew I'd never be able to come up with a good excuse for going to bed with my shoes on.

Dad took a step into the room.

My eye started to twitch. A nervous twitch.

I waited . . . and heard Dad snap off the light and shut our door.

Yes!

"Let's wait about an hour for Mom and Dad to go to sleep," Steve whispered. "Then we're going back out there. Because this is the last night you'll ever say the word *ghost* again!"

An hour later I was staring up at the tree house.

"Keep going," Steve ordered. "We're checking out every inch of it." He shoved me toward the rungs.

I didn't hear any creaks. Or any squealing nails. *That's a good sign,* I told myself. The ghost probably left.

But a tiny movement in the far corner of the

second level caught my eye. Then I saw a shadowy form move down to the first floor.

I dug my fingers into Steve's arm.

"Ow!" Steve complained.

"Do you see it?" I whispered. "Look!"

Steve peered up.

His eyes were glued to the tree house.

To the ghost who was waiting there.

13

"I don't see anything," Steve declared. "Now climb up."

"The ghost is there," I insisted. "It just moved down to the bottom platform."

"Great. I can't wait to meet it," Steve said. He gave me a hard shove.

"We can't just go barging up there," I whispered. "We don't want to make it angry. Remember what happened to that boy Duncan."

Duncan. Dylan. Even our names sounded alike. I couldn't help thinking I was going to be the next ghost of Fear Street.

"Yoohoo! Mr. Ghost, we're coming to visit," Steve whispered.

He thinks he's so funny. "You go first, since you think it's all such a big joke."

"Nope. This is your ghost."

I climbed the first rung of the ladder. Steve stood right behind me.

My mouth felt totally dry. I tried to swallow, but I couldn't.

Steve poked me in the back. "Come on," he said. "It's cold here. I'm freezing."

I climbed onto the second rung. Only three more to go. *You* want *to see a ghost,* I reminded myself. *But I'd rather see it from farther away,* I added.

Steve poked me again.

I felt around for the third rung of the ladder. Then I remembered. The old board was rotten and I hadn't hammered the new one on yet.

I reached up and grabbed the fifth rung.

Then my fingers slipped. And I crashed to the ground, taking Steve with me.

I moaned as the back of my head hit a rock. I tried to lift my head, but I felt too dizzy.

I slowly opened my eyes.

And saw *two* pale faces hovering above me.

Their eyes gleamed.

Their mouths hung open wide.

Ghosts! *Two* ghosts!

Their hands stretched toward me.

Reaching. Reaching.

"Stay away!" I shrieked.

Steve saw them, too. "Run, Dylan!" he cried. "Run!"

14

Two ghosts. How could there be two ghosts?

I struggled to my feet.

"Stay away!" I shrieked.

"Don't hurt me, please," Steve cried.

"Please leave us alone!" I begged.

"Ooooooh! Ooooooh!" one of the ghosts moaned.

"Please. Please," one ghost mocked.

"Don't hurt me, please," the other one chanted.

Then they started to giggle.

They didn't cackle or howl like ghosts. They giggled like girls.

Human girls.

Betsy and Kate.

They were stretched out on their stomachs with their heads hanging out the trapdoor.

"Please leave us alone!" Betsy laughed until she choked.

And here's the worst part. Steve was laughing, too.

"Ooooh, a ghost, I'm *sooo* scared," Steve said.

I felt my face burn. My hands clenched into fists. "You think this is funny?" I demanded. "You are all sick."

Kate clambered down the ladder. Betsy followed right behind her.

"You-you're the ones who have been playing all those tricks?" I stammered. "The hammer? The boards? Everything?"

"Well, yes," Betsy admitted. "You wouldn't listen to me when I tried to tell you the tree house was haunted. So we decided to haunt it ourselves."

No ghosts. Just dumb girls teasing me. It's the story of my life. I'm never going to see a real ghost. Never.

"We really fooled you, didn't we?" Kate exclaimed. She bounced up and down, her ponytail flying.

"I know you believed every word of my ghost story," Betsy chimed in.

"No, I didn't," I protested. "I wanted to keep an

open mind. Lots of scientists believe in ghosts, and—"

"Don't lie," Steve interrupted. "Admit it. They got you good."

"We spent half the day setting up that barricade around the tree," Betsy explained. "Good thing we're on vacation. Being ghosts is hard work."

Steve started to laugh again. "I told Dylan a million times there are no such things as ghosts. But does he listen to his older—"

"Shut up!" I yelled. "All of you. Just shut up."

"Don't be angry," Kate pleaded. "We knew you wanted to see a ghost . . . and so . . . and so . . ." She ruined her apology by bursting into giggles again.

"Come on, Dylan, my lad," Steve said in that big brother voice I hate. "I'll take you home. You've had quite a scare."

"Me! What about you? You screamed when you saw them, remember?" I was so mad I could barely get the words out.

"I did not scream. Like I always say, Dylan— there are no ghosts. Now let's go home. It's way past your bedtime."

Steve and I took off across the clearing. Kate and Betsy kept calling for us to come back. But no way. I couldn't face them.

I felt like a total jerk. I couldn't speak.

72

I just headed toward home with Steve.

As soon as we were through the clearing and hidden by the woods, Steve stopped and grabbed my arm. "I'm going to kill you, Dylan. You made us look like morons."

I jerked my arm away and shoved him. "How did I make you look like a moron?" I snapped. "You laughed your head off."

"Yeah, but thanks to you I was out there sneaking around looking for *ghosts.*"

"You're always telling me how much smarter you are. Why did you bother listening to me?" I asked.

That shut him up.

We walked the rest of the way back in silence. When we reached the house, Steve opened the door and said, "You're right. I'm never listening to you again."

We stepped into the kitchen. Steve leaned close to me and whispered, "Wake up Mom and Dad and you're dead meat."

"I'm sooo scared," I whispered back.

We crept through the kitchen and up the stairs to our room. I kicked off my shoes without bothering to untie them. Mom hates that, but I was too tired to care.

I climbed straight into bed.

But I couldn't fall asleep.

I kept hearing Kate and Betsy.

Giggling.

I hate them, I thought. *I really, really hate them.*

I rolled over onto my side. Then I tried my back. Then the other side. I couldn't get comfortable.

"Stop moving around up there," Steve grumbled. "I'm trying to sleep."

"I'm trying to sleep, too." Then I rolled over and made the bed shake as much as I could.

Steve growled.

I closed my eyes. And thought.

Then I bolted up in bed.

I know what would make me feel better!

I was going to get even with Betsy and Kate.

I was going to give them the worst scare of their lives.

Now I just had to figure out how.

15

The next day started out bad. And then got worse. Steve woke me up at five A.M. because it was raining. I had to deliver his newspapers when it rained. That was the deal.

The papers weighed a ton. I couldn't throw them on a porch from the curb. So I had to get off my bike at every house and run the paper to the door. In the rain.

When I returned home, Dad handed me a list of chores that he wanted Steve and me to do. A list a mile long. They would take the rest of the day—at least.

"After you finish these," he said, "you should be

pretty tired. Too tired to sneak out in the middle of the night."

Ha-ha, Dad.

Before I started chore number one—clean the garage—I wanted a bowl of Froot Loops. They're my favorite cereal. But the box was empty.

I knew Steve ate the last bowl—Mom and Dad hate Froot Loops. So does Steve. But he finished them because today was get-even-with-Dylan-day—for making him look like an idiot in front of the girls.

I headed out to the garage—wet *and* hungry. I was in a really bad mood now.

I found Steve reading a comic book. Of course he hadn't started the chores without me. I asked him why.

"Why should I," he said, "when everything was your fault?"

How did I make it through the morning without killing Steve? By imagining ways to get even with Betsy and Kate. As I sorted and stacked rolls of duct tape, electrical tape, and masking tape, I pictured myself taping Kate and Betsy's mouths shut.

That way they would never be able to fool anyone again with their stupid stories.

As I organized the paint cans along one wall, I imagined dumping paint over their heads, turning their black hair green or orange. Or green *and* orange.

By the time we had cleaned the whole garage, I'd come up with about a thousand awful things to do to them.

But none of them were right.

None of them were scary enough.

In the late afternoon, after all my chores were done, I decided to visit the tree house. Just one last time, I told myself.

I wasn't afraid of meeting a ghost anymore. Not there, anyway. I still believed in ghosts—don't get me wrong. But I didn't think the tree house was haunted —except by two stupid girls.

I circled the old oak, studying the work Steve and I had done. The tree house was coming out great. The first floor was complete, and we had begun work on the second level.

I found one of the boards that Betsy and Kate had pried loose. It was lying on the grass next to one of my cardboard boxes.

I brushed the dirt off it and picked up my hammer. Then I climbed up into the tree house and hammered it back into place.

I went back down for some more boards. I had trouble getting them up into the tree by myself, but somehow I managed.

Before I knew it, it was time for dinner—and I had built two entire walls!

"I'm going to finish this tree house," I muttered. "Even if I have to do it all by myself."

The tree house will be great when it's done, I thought as I made my way back home. *And those stupid girls will be really jealous. Because I won't let them anywhere near it.*

That night I sat on my bed and stared out the window. Still plotting my revenge.

That's when I spotted the lights. Lights coming from the direction of the tree house.

"You're not going to believe this, Steve!" I exclaimed.

"I'm not listening to you," Steve informed me, without bothering to look up from his comic book.

"Oh," I said. "So you aren't interested in the fact that the girls are back out by the tree house?"

Steve jumped up and charged over to the window. "I can't believe them!" he cried. "Even you aren't dumb enough to fall for their dumb trick two nights in a row."

That's when I came up with my idea.

The perfect idea for revenge.

"No, tonight they are going to fall for one of *our* tricks," I told Steve. "Put on a black shirt, black pants, black everything."

"How about a black eye for you?" my very mature brother replied. "Now leave me alone."

"Please, Steve," I begged. "You have to come with me. Just one last time. To get even with those girls."

Steve glanced out the window again. I could tell he was going to change his mind.

"What's the plan?" he asked.

"Tonight *we'll* be the ghosts of the tree house," I explained. "We'll sneak up on them and scare them to death!"

Steve smiled. He grabbed his black sweatshirt and pulled it over his head. "We'll scare them good."

In a few minutes we were both dressed in black. Steve even found a black baseball cap. We crept downstairs and into the backyard. We decided not to risk using flashlights.

We moved along the path slowly. We didn't want to make a sound. We wanted to surprise them.

It seemed as if it took forever but we finally reached the clearing.

Please let them still be there, I thought. *Please. Please. Please.*

I peered up at the tree house. And spotted a light on the first level.

Yes!

As we tiptoed closer to the tree house, every

sound thundered in my ears. My sneakers squeaking on the wet grass. Steve's breathing. My heart pounding.

Don't let them hear us, I thought. *Not now. Not when we're so close.*

We made it to the big rock next to the old oak and ducked behind it. I motioned to Steve that I would go up the ladder first. He'd follow right behind.

I carefully climbed the ladder. I made sure I had my weight balanced and my hands positioned on each rung before I took the next step. We were so close to success—I didn't want to ruin everything now.

One rung. Two. Three. Four. Only one more to go.

I climbed to the fifth rung.

I carefully reached up to the trapdoor.

I made sure I had a firm grip on it.

I glanced down to make sure Steve was in position behind me.

Then I flung open the door. And burst into the tree house with a loud howl.

But what I saw made me scream in terror.

I thought I would scream forever.

16

A ghost.

A real ghost.

It looked like a boy. A boy about my age. But I could see right through him.

As I leaped up through the trapdoor, he reached out to grab me. His icy fingers brushed my cheek.

I dodged his grasp and flung myself against the wall.

And then Steve jumped up into the tree house, howling his special werewolf howl. It turned into a whine when he spotted the ghost.

The ghost extended both his arms straight out. His hands were clenched in tight fists. I watched in horror as he slowly uncurled his fingers and pointed them at Steve.

A gust of icy wind blew up—up from the ghost's hands. It swept Steve off his feet and sent him *whooshing* toward me.

Then there was a loud *thud!* The thud of the trapdoor slamming shut.

Steve and I huddled together in the corner. I was sweating even though the room was freezing cold. Beads of sweat dripped down my forehead and into my eyes. I wanted to blink. But I didn't dare.

I didn't dare take my eyes off the ghost.

The ghost started to move toward us. He seemed to walk, but his feet never really touched the floor.

His eyes—his glowing red eyes—stared into mine. I lifted my hand to wipe the sweat from my forehead. The ghost's eyes flickered. I dropped my hand down to my side—fast.

I could feel Steve trembling beside me. "Wh-what do you think he's going to do?" he whispered.

I didn't answer. I couldn't. All I could do was stare. Stare into those terrifying eyes.

The ghost moved closer.

Closer.

He lifted his filmy white arms and began to reach out. Reach out for us.

His lips parted in an evil sneer.

The air around us grew colder. My teeth began to chatter.

Closer. Closer.

He was inches from us now.

Do something, do something, I told myself. Don't just stand there. *DO SOMETHING!*

I leaped around the ghost and lunged across the room. Across to the trapdoor.

I slid on my stomach and grabbed for the handle. I began to pull, but it slipped out of my sweaty hand.

The ghost howled in fury. He rose up in the air.

I scrambled up on my knees and grabbed the handle again.

"Hurry, Dylan!" Steve screamed. "Hurry!"

The ghost swooped down.

I jerked the door open.

The ghost flew right at me. Then he flew right through me. He hovered over my head. I froze in sheer terror.

I stared up into his eyes. They glowed an angry red.

He floated close to me. I could feel his icy breath on my neck. Then he reached down and banged the trapdoor hard. It slammed shut.

"Don't move," he howled. "You're not going anywhere ever again."

83

17

"**Y**ou're not going anywhere ever again," the ghost repeated. "I can't let you leave. Not yet."

I shot a glance at Steve, but he sat shriveled up in the corner. His mouth gaped open and his hands and legs trembled. *He's not going to be much help here,* I thought.

"What do you want?" I managed to ask.

"I need your help," the ghost said.

"Help? What help? Who are you?" I was actually talking to a ghost!

He looked just like a regular kid. A regular kid I could see right through.

"My name is Corey—or it was Corey when I was alive. . . ." the ghost replied softly.

When I was alive.

"So you're really a ghost," I said to Corey—but I was staring at Steve.

"How does it feel to be a ghost?" I blurted out. I had so many questions. Now was my chance to get some answers. Especially since the ghost wasn't letting us go anywhere.

"I guess it feels like being asleep," he began to explain. "I'm not exactly sure. You see, this is my first day as a ghost. Before this I was trapped in this tree house—without any shape at all. But you changed all that."

"I-I did?" I asked.

"Yes," the ghost replied. "The more you worked on the tree house, the stronger I grew. Now I can move around. I can see again. I haven't been able to do that since I died. And I have a voice and a body—well, sort of a body. But I still can't leave the tree house. I'm still too weak."

"H-how did you become a ghost?" I asked.

"I died in this tree house," he replied. "In a lightning storm."

"Wow! Steve, did you hear that? The story is true," I cried.

Steve didn't say anything. To tell you the truth, I think he was in shock.

But I wasn't afraid at all. The ghost didn't seem scary. He just seemed sad. Sad and lonely.

"You said you need our help," I whispered. "What do you want us to do?"

"I want you to finish building the tree house," the ghost explained. "I've been trapped in this tree house where I died—for years and years. But if you finish the tree house, I'm sure I'll be strong enough to leave here."

That's all? That's easy! It's almost finished anyway, I thought.

"Will you help me?" the ghost asked again.

"Yeah. We'll help you," Steve interrupted before I could answer. "But we want to make a deal."

"A deal?" The ghost boy's voice sounded cold and hard. He floated over to Steve—and seeing him hover in the air made my body clench with fear.

"Why should I make a deal with *you?*" he bellowed.

18

I couldn't believe it! I'd been doing all the talking while my very mature brother hid in the corner. And now he wanted to make a deal!

Steve's going to ruin everything. We'll never get out of here alive.

I glared at Steve. "We don't have to make—"

Steve cut me off again. "We'll help you on one condition," he declared. "You have to help us get even with two girls."

"And you'll finish the tree house—no delays?" the ghost said.

"Yes," I said eagerly.

"Then I will help you," the ghost said.

"Deal," Steve replied. "Now here's the plan. . . ."

The next week Steve and I worked every day after school on the tree house.

Steve didn't read one comic book.

He didn't make one trip back to the house for Cheese Curlies.

I didn't even have to bribe him with doughnuts.

And now it was Saturday—and we were just about finished. The tree house looked awesome.

"Steve, I need some more nails," I called from the roof.

"Here, Dylan. Catch!" Steve threw a handful of nails at me. They flew over the roof and landed on the ground. Steve was turning back into his old self.

"Why do you have to act like such a jerk?" I shouted.

"Dylan, my lad, I can't wait until we're finished with the tree house. Then I'll never have to see you again."

"We still share a room," I replied.

"Not for long," Steve answered.

"Why?" I asked. "Are you going somewhere?"

"Nope," Steve answered. "You are."

"I don't think so, Steve."

"Oh, yes, you are. It's part of the deal I made with the ghost. You're moving into the tree house.

88

Corey needs someone to take over haunting the tree house. I told him you would do it. You like ghosts so much, I figured you wouldn't mind becoming one."

"How could you do this to me?" I yelled. "I'm not doing it!"

"A deal's a deal, Dylan, my lad," Steve answered. Then he started to laugh. "Boy, you'll believe anything!"

I was ready to throw my hammer at Steve, but I stopped when I heard voices down below.

Girls' voices.

Betsy and Kate.

"They're here," I whispered to Steve.

"I knew they would show up," Steve whispered back.

"Wow!" Kate said as she and Betsy approached the old oak. "The tree house is almost finished."

"Yeah. Your dumb tricks didn't work," I mumbled under my breath.

Kate and Betsy walked around the tree house slowly, studying it. "It looks really good," Kate finally said. "I'll bet this is what it looked like when it was first built."

Betsy nodded. "It's not bad," she said. "But you're lucky you didn't get hurt."

I opened my mouth to start to tell them off. But Kate cut me off.

"Maybe those terrible stories we heard weren't true. Maybe someone was trying to trick us," she said.

Yeah. Sure. Right, I thought.

"Listen," Steve said. "Why don't the four of us try to be friends from now on? We're going to have a party up here tonight. To celebrate finishing the tree house. Want to come?"

Kate and Betsy didn't answer right away. Kate started nibbling on her ponytail.

"Sure," Betsy finally agreed.

"Great," Steve said. "We'll meet here after dark. It'll be fun!"

The girls left.

Steve and I finished hammering in the last nails on the tree house roof. Then we climbed down and inspected our work from every angle.

The tree house looked really awesome!

We dashed home, gulped down dinner, and collected stuff for the party—chips, soda, things like that.

As soon as it grew dark out, we headed back through the woods. I had gotten used to it being so quiet out here. The Fear Street Woods didn't frighten me anymore.

Steve and I climbed the ladder and set out everything for the party.

Steve popped a Cheese Curlie in his mouth and

walked over to the tree house window. "Here they come!" he whispered.

We could hear the girls climbing the ladder. Steve pulled open the trapdoor for them. "Come on in," he called.

Betsy peeked her head through the door first. Kate was right behind her.

"What do you think?" I asked as they glanced around the first level.

Betsy remained silent. Kate's eyes looked as if they were about to pop right out of her head. "Wow! It really turned out great," she finally said.

The girls plopped down on the floor. I started to pour soda for everyone.

And that's when we heard it.

A soft moan.

"Wh-what was that?" Kate asked.

"Probably just the wind," Steve replied.

Then we heard it again.

Louder this time. And creepier. Almost like a wail.

Betsy grabbed Kate's hand. "We're leaving," she declared.

She moved to the trapdoor, bent down, and grasped its handle.

But before she could pull it open, an icy wind blew through the tree house, sending everything soaring through the air.

The chips whirled around the room. Cups of soda flew up and splattered against the wall.

Steve and I braced ourselves on the floor.

Betsy's knuckles turned white as she gripped the trapdoor handle. Her eyes were wide with fright.

And then Corey sprang up—right through the trapdoor. He let out the most hideous shriek I've ever heard.

The girls screamed their heads off.

Corey stretched himself to twice his normal size. He really was much stronger—now that we'd finished the house for him.

He swung his filmy arms wildly and the icy wind blew stronger. His eyes glowed like red embers. And his mouth gaped open—showing rows and rows of rotted, black teeth.

Steve laughed like a maniac. His plan had worked—the girls were getting the worst scare of their lives.

I stared at the girls as they shrieked and shrieked. They couldn't stop.

And then I saw something.

Something that made my breath catch in my throat.

Something that made my heart stop.

19

Betsy and Kate rose up in the air.

Up to join Corey.

As I watched, the color faded from their bodies. Their black hair turned a misty white. Their eyes began to glow a deep red.

My heart pounded. I thought my chest was going to explode.

The girls wrapped their arms around Corey. And they hugged!

"They're ghosts, too!" I howled. "They're ghosts, too!"

Steve raised his eyes to the weird scene. I heard him give a low groan.

The three ghosts cackled and danced in the air. They spun around and around.

Cold air shot through me as they flew past. My teeth started to chatter.

"Run!" Steve screamed. "Run!"

I flung open the trapdoor.

As we slid down the trunk I could feel my skin ripping open against the rough bark. It didn't matter. Nothing mattered except getting away— fast.

We bolted across the clearing toward the woods.

We nearly reached the path.

And then the ghosts swooped down on us.

They joined hands and surrounded us. Surrounded us in an icy circle of air.

My whole body trembled as the ghosts whirled around us. Faster and faster. And laughing—evil, hideous laughs.

Corey swung in front of me and grinned in triumph.

And then the ghosts began to move in.

Closer and closer.

Tightening the circle.

Until we were trapped.

20

"**W**e have to get out of here—now!" I screamed to Steve.

Steve and I flung ourselves at the ghosts. But the ghosts bounced us right back. Back to the center of the circle.

I tried again. I flew at the filmy creatures with all my might.

This time they caught me. I was stuck right between two quivering, icy ghosts. I felt as if I were being smothered in freezing-cold Jell-O.

I started to shiver. My arms and legs shook and my teeth chattered. My lips began to turn numb.

I couldn't breathe. I started to choke. I was freezing. Freezing to death.

It was all a trick, I thought. A horrible trick. Corey made us finish the tree house. And now he's going to kill us.

Steve sank to the ground and curled up in a little ball. I clenched my fists and threw myself against the ghosts. I pushed and pushed. Then with one last burst of strength, I shoved against them hard.

I was out! I doubled over, gulping down air. I could breathe again. And I was free!

I straightened up—and that's when I realized the awful truth. I was still inside the circle.

"You can't keep me here!" I screamed, running forward again—pushing against the clammy cold that surrounded me.

Betsy shrieked with laughter. Corey laughed, too.

"Stop! Stop! Can't you see they're scared?" It was Kate.

The laughter died.

Then Betsy spoke.

"I'm sorry," she said. "We were just playing. We didn't mean to scare you."

"Yeah," Corey added. "I guess we got carried away."

Carried away? This must be a bad dream, I thought. A really bad dream.

"Corey is our brother," Kate began. "We thought we would never find him."

My mouth dropped open.

I glanced at Steve. He sat shriveled up on the ground, staring into space.

"Corey, Betsy, and I were the three kids in the tree house—the kids we told you about," Kate continued. "When the tree house was hit by lightning, Betsy and I were on one side of it. Corey was on the other side."

"We all died at the same time," Betsy said, taking up the story. "When we became ghosts, Kate and I were together. But Corey disappeared. His spirit was lost. We've been searching for him ever since."

Kate waited for me to say something. But I didn't. I was afraid to speak. I was afraid to move. I was too afraid to do anything but listen.

"When you discovered the tree house," she went on, "we suddenly found ourselves back in these woods. We *thought* we had been brought back to scare you away from it. So you wouldn't get hurt— the way we did."

"But now we know we were wrong," Betsy interrupted. "We must have been brought back to find Corey. And you two helped us!"

"Thank you. Thank you so much," Corey added. "You freed me from the tree house. Finally!"

"Yes!" Betsy exclaimed. "We would never have found Corey without you!"

As she spoke a ray of moonlight broke through

the thick treetops. It cast a golden glow on the three ghosts.

"I-I guess I believe you," I stammered.

"We're telling the truth," Kate replied. "Really."

"I-I guess this could be kind of cool," I stuttered. "You'll be able to tell me everything I ever wanted to know about ghosts. I can come out to the tree house every day and you can—"

"Sorry, Dylan," Corey interrupted me. "We've been stuck on earth a long time. You brought us together. Now we can leave."

And with that, the beam of moonlight began to shimmer. Steve and I watched in awe as it expanded to form a wide, sparkling bridge. It stretched from the moon all the way down to the clearing. It was the most beautiful thing I had ever seen.

The three ghosts reached out and touched Steve and me one last time. Their fingers felt soft and fluttery, like a gentle breeze. As we looked at them, they started to fade and become even more transparent.

Then they joined hands and stepped onto the bridge of light. Kate glanced back and waved.

They walked on the shimmering moonbeam.

Up toward the sky.

And then they disappeared.

"Can you believe that?" I asked Steve. "Can you believe that!"

Steve still couldn't speak. But he did manage to nod "yes."

"Well, well, well, Steve, my lad. You finally believe in ghosts!"

21

I felt dazed after the ghosts disappeared. I turned and followed Steve home. With our three friends gone, I also felt strange. Kind of alone.

I walked close to Steve. The woods seemed darker than ever.

Twigs crackled loudly under our shoes. I heard animal moans and strange cries.

Steve stopped. He spun around. "Hey—where are we?"

Nothing looked familiar. "I-I think we went the wrong way," I stammered. I searched for the moon, but trees blocked the light.

"Those ghosts got me all mixed up," Steve

confessed. He turned and pointed. "I think the path is over there."

I followed him, but I couldn't see any path.

Then, in a small, round clearing, I saw a strange sight. Silvery moonlight spilled into the clearing. And in the moonlight, I saw an old swing set. An old-fashioned wooden swing and slide. Worn and rickety-looking.

And on top of the swing set sat a boy. He had long blond curls that shone in the moonlight. He was dressed in a sailor suit, the kind you see kids wearing in very old pictures.

He was so pale. The moonlight seemed to pour right through him.

Was he stuck up there on that battered swing set?

"Help me," he called when Steve and I stepped into the clearing, into the spotlight of silvery moonlight. "Please—help me!"

Steve and I both rolled our eyes and shook our heads. "Here we go again!" I moaned.

Are you ready for another walk
down Fear Street?
Turn the page for a terrifying
sneak preview.

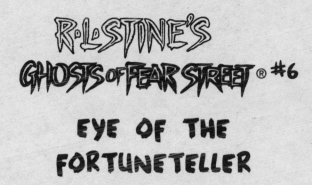

R·L·STINE'S
GHOSTS of FEAR STREET ® #6

EYE OF THE
FORTUNETELLER

Coming mid-February 1996

"**F**ortunetellers are fakes. Everyone knows that. They can't really tell the future," Drew argued, trying to convince his cousin.

But Kelsey ignored him. She pulled the door to the fortuneteller's shack open wide enough to stick her head inside. The air inside the shack felt icy cold. It sent a chill down her spine.

She glanced around the room. A layer of thick dust carpeted the floor. Old books were scattered everywhere.

Kelsey's gaze shifted to the far wall of the shack, where bookshelves rose from the floor to the ceiling. On them sat tons and tons of stuffed animals.

Kelsey stared at the animals. They weren't like the ones she had in her room.

These were real animals.

Real dead animals.

"You're not going to believe what's in here," Kelsey whispered. "Let's go in."

"No way!" Drew said. Then he tugged Kelsey back. "Let's go. We'll be here all summer. We can come back another time."

Kelsey sighed. "Oh, all right, but—"

"Stay. Stay," a raspy voice called from the back of the shack.

Kelsey and Drew turned in time to see a very old woman make her way to the front of the shack. She pointed a wrinkled, gnarled finger at them. "Come," she said. "Come in."

Kelsey stared at the woman. She wore a red flowered dress that hung down to the floor. Her face was lined with wrinkles. And her mouth twisted in a half sneer. But it was her earrings that Kelsey gaped at.

Dozens of gold rings dangled from each ear. Heavy gold earrings that pulled on her lobes and made them hang low.

She fixed her dark eyes on Kelsey as she spoke again.

Kelsey gasped. The woman had one blue eye and one eye the color of coal.

"Come," the woman beckoned. "Come inside. There is much to tell. Come, Kelsey and Drew."

All the color drained from Drew's face. "Kelsey, how does she know our names?" he murmured. "How does she know?"

"She probably heard us talking," Kelsey whispered to Drew.

"But we just walked around the shack. She wasn't there," he replied.

"Maybe she heard us through the windows or something," Kelsey answered. "Trust me, these fortunetellers are all fakes. You said so yourself."

"Come, children," the gypsy woman continued, opening the door wider. "Come inside." Then she gazed over her shoulder. "I have something for you."

"Um, thanks. But we can't," Drew said. "We really have to get home."

The gypsy ignored him. And so did Kelsey. She followed the old woman inside. Drew lunged for Kelsey's arm and tried to pull her back, but Kelsey jerked free.

"You have some pretty neat things in here," Kelsey said to the woman as she stepped inside.

"These are not my things," she replied. Then she sat down behind a round table. "Sit." She motioned to two chairs. "You may call me Madame Valda."

"I thought she was supposed to be the Amazing Zandra," Drew whispered as the two took their seats at the table.

Kelsey shrugged as she watched the gypsy set a folded velvet cloth on the table in front of her. It was bloodred and held something inside it.

"Madame Valda will tell your fortune now," the gypsy announced. Then she opened the cloth to reveal a deck of cards.

"But we don't have any money to pay you, uh, Madame Gypsy," Drew said, standing.

"Madame *Valda,*" the old woman corrected sharply. Then her voice softened. "I will do it for nothing. Sit! It is a great honor to have Madame Valda tell your fortune."

"Sit!" Kelsey echoed.

Drew sat. Madame Valda spread the deck of cards out on the table. She began to sing softly in a language Kelsey had never heard.

Kelsey watched as the fortuneteller swirled her head around in a circle. She'd seen fortunetellers in the movies do this. They closed their eyes and sang themselves into some kind of trance.

Only Madame Valda didn't close her eyes.

She stared straight ahead. Straight at Kelsey.

This is really creepy, Kelsey thought. A nervous giggle escaped her lips.

Madame Valda didn't seem to notice—or she didn't care.

She continued to sing.

She continued to stare.

Directly into Kelsey's eyes.

Kelsey stared back. She felt as if she were in some kind of trance, too. She couldn't stop gazing into the woman's weird eyes.

Finally Madame Valda's chant came to an end, and she shifted her gaze to the deck of cards on the table.

Kelsey let out a long sigh. She didn't realize she'd been holding her breath.

Madame Valda flipped over three cards. They all had strange symbols on them. Symbols that Kelsey had never seen before.

The gypsy studied the cards for a moment, then turned to Drew.

"Drew Foster," she said. "I see that you are sometimes more a follower than a leader. You must be careful to guard against that. It will get you into trouble. Especially when you let Kelsey make all the decisions."

Kelsey shot a quick glance at Drew. His jaw dropped and his eyes grew wide.

Kelsey squirmed in her chair. *How did she know Drew's last name?* she wondered. *How?* Kelsey knew she never said it. And neither did Drew. Not outside. And not inside.

Then she spotted it. Drew's beach pass. Pinned to his shirt. With his name printed in big red letters, Drew T. Foster. Kelsey laughed out loud as she stared down at her own badge. Then she pointed it out to Drew.

"What is funny?" the old woman snarled.

"Um. Nothing," Kelsey replied.

"Then why do you laugh?" the old woman pressed.

"Well, it's just that your fortunetelling powers

aren't all that, um, mysterious," Kelsey confessed.

Drew kicked Kelsey under the table.

"Do you think Madame Valda is a fake?" The old woman's voice rose to a screech.

"I *know* Madame Valda is a fake," Kelsey replied, imitating the gypsy's accent.

"You have insulted the famous Madame Valda!" the fortuneteller roared. She jerked to her feet and loomed over Kelsey. "Apologize now, or live the rest of your life in fear."

"In fear of what?" Kelsey asked, staring directly into Madame Valda's dark eye. "I'm not afraid of you."

"Oh, yes, you are!" Madame Valda cried. "I am the most powerful fortuneteller who ever lived. And I know all your fears, you foolish child. All your fears!"

"Just say you're sorry and let's go," Drew said, pushing his chair from the table. Then he added in a whisper, "She's worse than scary—she's nuts."

"No," Kelsey told Drew. "I am *not* afraid."

Madame Valda's eyes flickered. She leaned in, closer to Kelsey. Kelsey could feel the gypsy's hot breath on her face. Then she whispered, "Only a fool is not afraid."

Before Kelsey could reply, the old woman reached down and flipped over the next card in the deck. She threw it down onto the table in front of Kelsey.

It looked like a joker.

Kelsey read the words on the bottom of the card—the Fool.

"The cards never lie! You are the fool, and I curse you for the rest of your life. Now get out!" she cried. "Get out. Now!"

Kelsey and Drew jumped up and bolted for the door. Madame Valda's voice thundered behind them. "You will believe. You will know *fear*."

As soon as their feet hit the boardwalk, Kelsey and Drew broke into a run.

But Madame Valda's voice trailed after them. "Fear! Fear! Fear!" she cried out over their pounding sneakers. "You will know fear!"

Kelsey and Drew ran faster. But Madame Valda's voice seemed as close as before. Kelsey glanced back. "Oh, no!" she cried. "She *is* crazy! She's coming after us!"

Kelsey's heart pounded as she ran faster.

Her lungs felt as if they were about to explode.

She turned back—and there was Madame Valda. Right behind her!

This is unreal, Kelsey's mind whirled. How could an old lady run so fast?

"She's right behind us!" Drew cried out, panting.

"Leave us alone!" Kelsey screamed over her shoulder.

Madame Valda's right eye burned into Kelsey—and Kelsey stopped running.

"Run! Run!" Drew screamed.

But Kelsey couldn't move. She felt paralyzed. Frozen in place by the dark eye of the fortune-teller.

The gypsy reached out and clutched Kelsey's shoulder with her bony fingers. A sharp pain shot down Kelsey's arm. She tried to jerk away, but Madame Valda held her tightly.

The old gypsy laughed. A hideous laugh.

"Not afraid!" she cackled. "Oh, yes. You will be afraid!" She whisked the Fool card before Kelsey's eyes, then tossed it in the air.

"Fool! Fool! Fool!" she cried. "Only a fool is not afraid!"

Kelsey and Drew watched as the card flew up. And up. And up. Until it faded to a white flicker in the sky. Then it was gone.

Kelsey wrenched free of Madame Valda's grip, and she and Drew flew down the boardwalk. She ran so fast, her lungs burned in her chest. She quickly glanced back—to see if the fortuneteller was still following them.

But Madame Valda was gone.

"Drew! Stop!" Kelsey grabbed her cousin's arm. "Look! Madame Valda. She disappeared."

Drew spun around. Kelsey was right. Madame Valda had simply vanished.

"How did she run so fast?" Drew asked, out of breath.

"I don't know," Kelsey replied, shaking her head. "Do you think she really was a fortuneteller? I mean, a *real* fortuneteller? With *real* powers?"

"Come on, Kelsey," Drew replied. "Now you sound as crazy as that old hag."

"Yeah, you're right," Kelsey said. But she didn't sound as if she meant it. "So, um, you don't think she put a curse on us, right?" Kelsey asked.

"Not on me," Drew answered. "I was nice to her, remember?"

"Thanks a lot." Kelsey punched Drew in the arm.

"Come on, Kelsey," Drew said. "She probably isn't even a real gypsy."

Kelsey knew that Drew was probably right. But she kept picturing the fortuneteller's strange eyes. And she kept hearing her voice. That horrible voice screaming, "Fool! Fool! Fool!"

About R. L. Stine

R. L. Stine, the creator of *Ghosts of Fear Street,* has written almost 100 scary novels for kids. The *Ghosts of Fear Street* series, like the *Fear Street* series, takes place in Shadyside and centers on the scary events that happen to people on Fear Street.

When he isn't writing, R. L. Stine likes to play pinball on his very own pinball machine, and explore New York City with his wife, Jane, and fifteen-year-old son, Matt.